Pieces and Parts

by Michele Gerber

For information regarding permission, write to:
Round Circle, Inc., P.O. Box 536822, Orlando, FL 32853

ISBN 978-0-9896306-0-3

Published by Round Circle, Inc.

Printed in USA

For Carson, Marley and You!

Pieces and parts, spackle and glue,

and that is how
I made you.

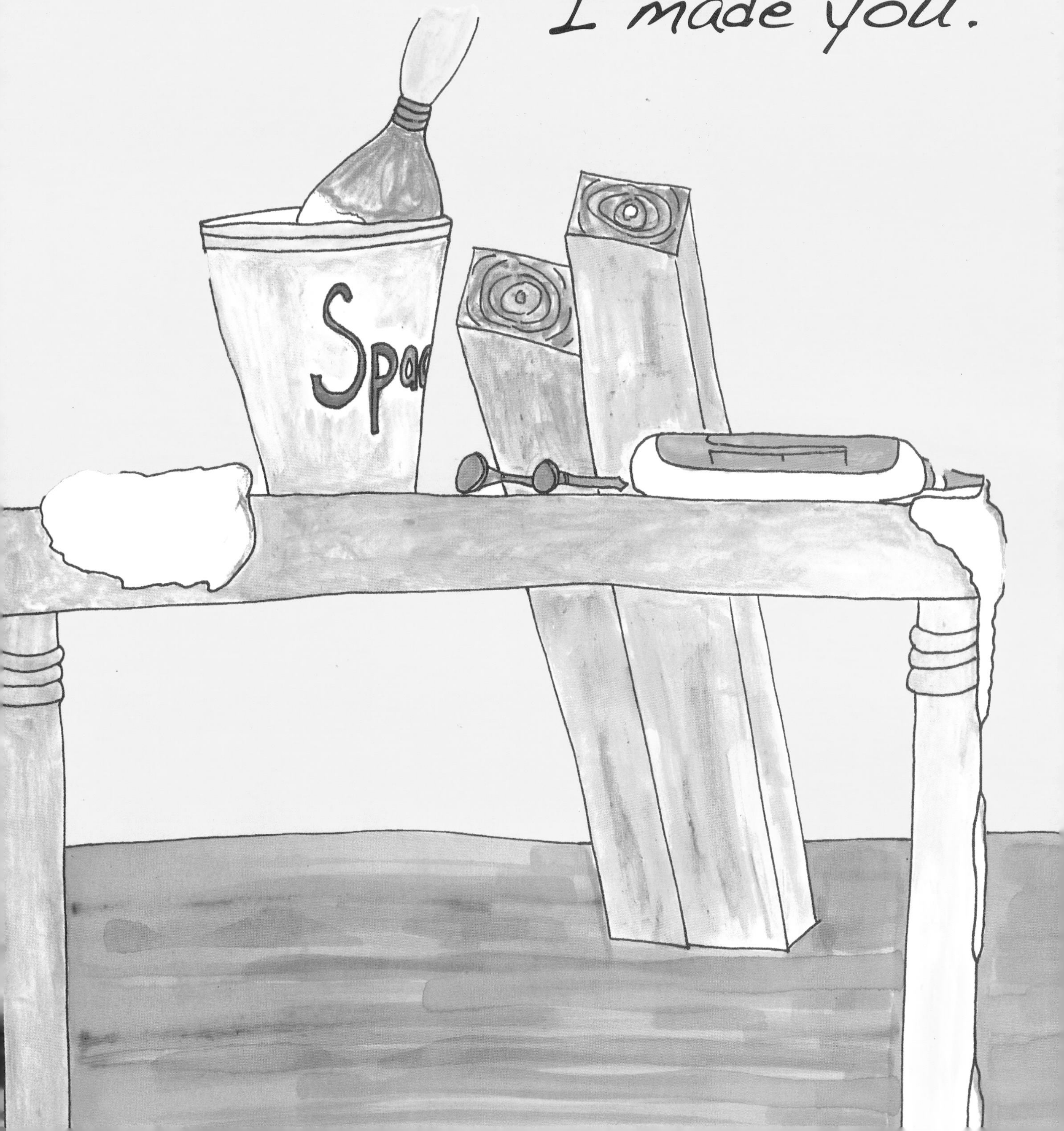

With lightning bugs,
electrical plugs,
and 12 ounces
of
slimy slugs.

A touch of class, a
and just enou

Fuzzies
and flowers

promise

laughter

for hours.

Glitter!

You must have glitter,

a lot of glitter,

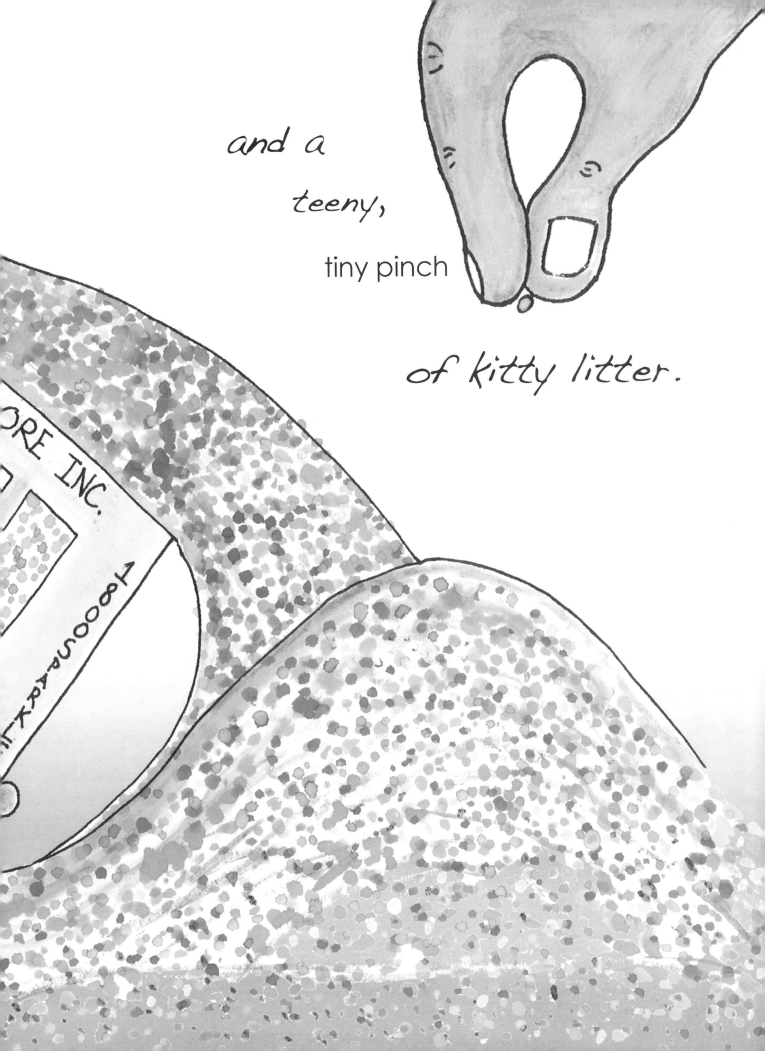

A buck,

a duck,

and a lot of luck
will help you when
you get
stuck.

I am giving you my 2 cents,
a white picket fence,

and believe me
   I've spared no expense.

Now, this may look like

plain old junk,

but with $\dfrac{1}{3}$ gunk and $\dfrac{2}{3}$ funk,

it will generate **1** with perfect

It has been foretold,
you BROKE
the **MOLD**,

but, *please*,
put on your socks

or you may catch cold!

A grass skirt,
a short sleeve shirt,
and elbow pads
so you
don't
get
hurt!

You can strut your stuff
for blocks,
when your hair totally rocks!

Can you say

feathers
à la
peacocks?

These shoes are smooth.

They'll help you move

. right into your

very own GROOVE.

Oh my gosh,
I forgot the final part.
It comes from
deep inside my heart.

We are going to

need another cart.

No matter
what it seems,
you have the means,
to capture
100 rainbows
worth of dreams.

There is no one else with these pieces and parts.

You are an
Original Work of Art.

You are a Masterpiece!

Place your picture here.

Masterpiece!

Spac